Hungry for Science:

Poems to Crunch On

Hungry for Science:
Poems to Crunch On

Kari-Lynn Winters & Lori Sherritt-Fleming

Illustrated by Peggy Collins

Fitzhenry & Whiteside

Published in Canada by Fitzhenry & Whiteside 195 Allstate Parkway, Markham, ON L3R 4T8

Published in the United States by Fitzhenry & Whiteside 311 Washington Street, Brighton, MA 02135

All inquiries should be addressed to Fitzhenry & Whiteside, 195 Allstate Parkway, Markham, ON. L3R 4T8

www.fitzhenry.ca

Fitzhenry & Whiteside acknowledges with thanks the Canada Council for the Arts and the Ontario Arts Council for their support of our publishing program.

We acknowledge the financial support of the Government of Canada through the Canada Book Fund (CBF) for our publishing activities.

Library and Archives Canada Cataloguing in Publication

Winters, Kari-Lynn, 1969-, author Sherritt-Fleming, Lori, 1968-, author Hungry for science : poems to crunch on /
Kari-Lynn Winters & Lori Sherritt-Fleming ; illustrated by Peggy Collins.

ISBN 978-1-55455-396-9 (hardcover)

1. Science--Juvenile poetry. 2. Children's poetry, Canadian (English).
I. Winters, Kari-Lynn, 1969-, author, Sherritt-Fleming, Lori, 1968-, author II. Collins, Peggy, illustrator
III. Title. Hungry for science : poems to crunch on

PS8645.I5745H86 2018   jC811′.6   C2018-901180-7

Publisher Cataloging-in-Publication Data (U.S.)

Names: Winters, Kari-Lynn, 1969-, author. | Sherritt-Fleming, Lori, 1968-, author. | Collins, Peggy, 1975-, illustrator.
Title: Hungry for Science : Poems to Crunch On / Kari-Lynn Winters & Lori Sherritt-Fleming ; illustrated by Peggy Collins.
Description: Markham, Ontario : Fitzhenry & Whiteside, 2018. | Summary: "A collection of fun and educational poems illustrating various science concepts." – Provided by publisher.
Identifiers: ISBN 978-1-55455-396-9 (hardcover)
Subjects: LCSH: Children's poetry, Canadian. | Science – Juvenile poetry. | BISAC: JUVENILE NONFICTION / Poetry / General.
Classification: LCC PR9199.3W568Hu | DDC 811.6 – dc23

Text and cover design by Kerry Designs
Cover illustration courtesy of Peggy Collins
Printed and bound in China by Sheck Wah Tong Printing Press Ltd.

10 9 8 7 6 5 4 3 2 1

Hungry for Science

She's hungry for science.
A science guru
turning solids to liquids
to gases too.

Magnets attract her
repel her as well.
She'll plant flower gardens
magnify a cell.

She'll study steel structures
create a kazoo
explore all the seasons
and dissolve drain pipe goo.

She's hungry for science.
Her hunger's so great.
Stirring her mixtures
who'd guess that she's eight?

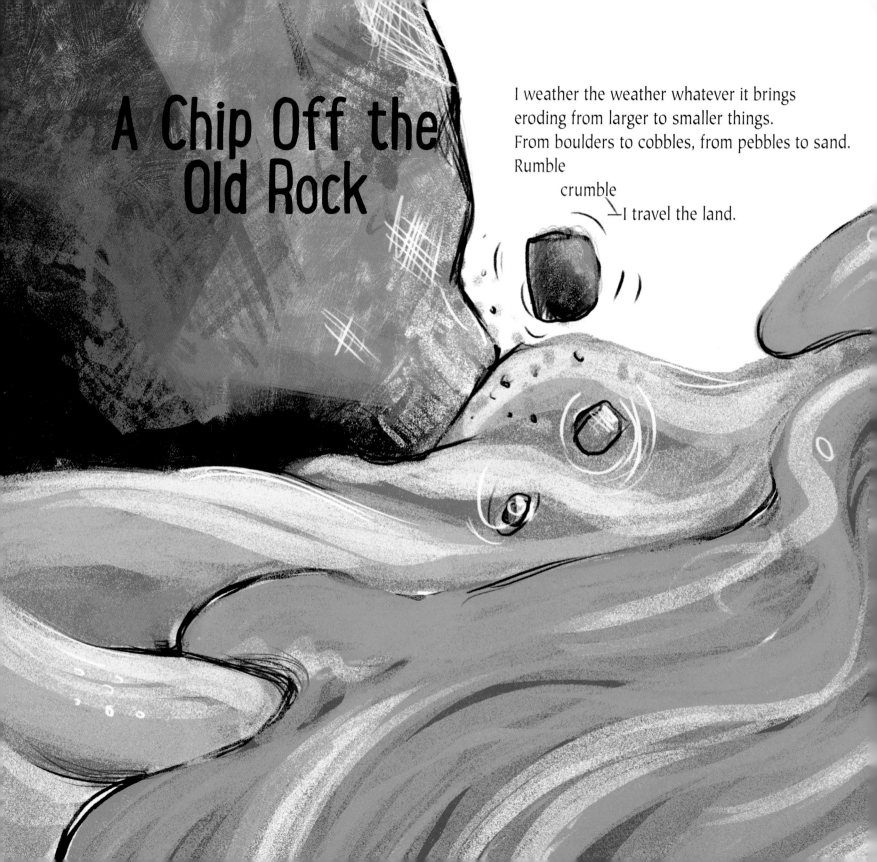

A Chip Off the Old Rock

I weather the weather whatever it brings
eroding from larger to smaller things.
From boulders to cobbles, from pebbles to sand.
Rumble
      crumble
        I travel the land.

Moving steadily down a steep slope
pushed by ice (to warm places I hope).
Tumbled by rivers I scramble downstream.

Blown by the wind—it's all part of my dream!
Deposited gently, I've come from good stock.
I know I'm a chip off an igneous rock.

A House Like That

2nd Pig:
Grassy stalks of dried grain
get all mouldy in the rain.
Who wants a house like that?
Sticks, sticks are where it's at!

An Ode to Flea

Little Miss Pesky Flea
passed at last
at half past three.

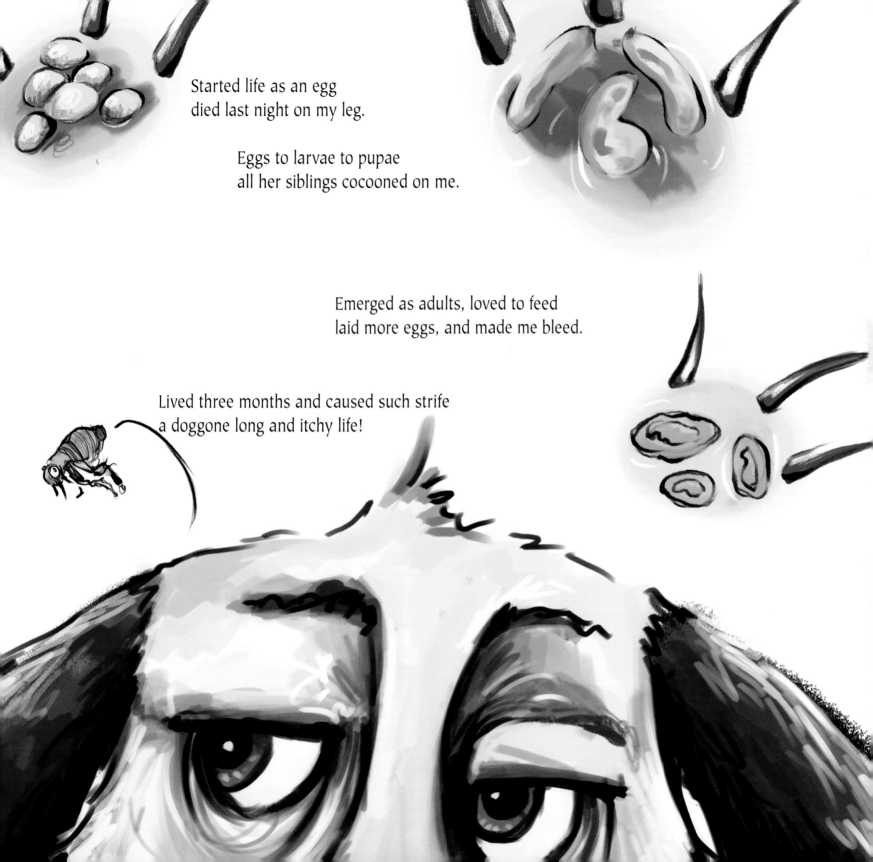

Started life as an egg
died last night on my leg.

Eggs to larvae to pupae
all her siblings cocooned on me.

Emerged as adults, loved to feed
laid more eggs, and made me bleed.

Lived three months and caused such strife
a doggone long and itchy life!

Captain
Chemistry
Saves the Da[y]

It's my turn to wash the dishes.
The sink is full of goo.
The drain pipe must be clogged again.
Whatever can I do?

Rat-a-tatty-bang-bang!
There's someone at the door.
It's Captain Chemistry.
He'll save the day for sure!

"Fear not," called the Captain
"I know just what to do!
Find some baking soda
And some vinegar too!"

Bubble-bubble-fizz-fizz.
They frothed as they mixed.
The fizziness created
soon had the drain-pipe fixed!

Hurray for the Captain!
The King of Chemistry!
His all-purpose cleaner
is also earth friend-ly!

Cycles

Cycles, cycles 'round and 'round
like wheels upon a bike.

Winter, spring, summer, fall—
which season do you like?

The earth moves 'round the sun
bringing winter snow.

Some months later, moving still
spring flowers start to grow.

The earth moves 'round the sun
bringing summer heat.

Some months later, moving still
we have fall fruit to eat.

Magnetic Attraction

Our particles are charged.
I'm DRAWN to YOU.
You're the North to my South.
You know that it's true.

It can't be stopped—
it's magnetic attraction!
Pulling you close—
a *can't fight it* reaction.

The force is too strong.
There's no way to yield.
Opposites attract—
a magnetic force field!

But wait…

you're getting too near

uncomfortably close
too near to my ear
too close to my mou—

This is what happens when North meets South?
Ew. Gross!

The SENSE-ational Brain

Whispered in your ear.
Tickled on your skin.
Taking sensations from the outside in.

Nerve cell to nerve cell—in a long chain.
Messages pulsed
to the brain.

Making sense
as they enter.
Your BRAIN—the body's CONTROL CENTRE.

Ring Zing Pound

Toot, hoot, trumpet, bleat.
Waves transport a steady beat.

Ring, zing, clatter, strum.
Noises vibrate each eardrum.

Crash, smash, rattle, pound.
Brains interpret to make sound.

What a clamour, never bland—
all from a one-man marching band.

Scary Miss Mary's Garden Tour

"Scary Miss Mary, the neighbours are wary
of how your odd garden grows.
With carnivorous snappers and large creepy wra
and that stinky, zombie-faced rose."

"My plot is botanic, rare, and organic.
My plants start as most do from seeds.
With soil, water, and sun, their lives newly begur
they germinate then spread like WEEDS!

Seeds send out roots and soon a stem shoots
to the sky with a JAB and a PROD!
New leaves unfurl and like tentacles whirl
'round your ANKLES—so watch where you've tr

Step lively now, friend. It's not
　　quite the end.
There's much more to my tour
　　than this.
In front of your eyes, plants
　　pho-to-syn-the-size.
(Oh excuse the horrible hiss.)

What? Leaving so soon? It's
　　barely past noon.
You'll REGRET not smelling
　　my flowers.
If pollination is speedy, they
　　become rather SEEDY.
A new cycle begins within hours.

"MWA! HA! HA!"

"Thank you Miss Mary but I must not tarry
in your garden on such a fine day.
I've learned a bunch but I have a hunch

An Elephant in the Classroom

There's an elephant in our classroom!
Halfway in and halfway out.
While squeezing through the doorway
he got stuck beyond a doubt.

"Things in motion stay in motion.
Things at rest—rest.
We must use force to move this
beast," called out Arabest.

"Gravity might help him if he falls through the floor!"
Gustav jumped up and down but the ground gave no more.

"Pull him gently by the trunk," proposed Aidan John.
His friends lined up and tried but no one could hang on.

"Push him backwards," offered Claire, "I'll coax him backwards too.
If we all work together he might just burst right through!"

They sweated and strained though their muscles were drained
and gave him a final...
        HEAVE!
                By the end of the class that great
                        pachyderm mass
                                could finally, happily leave!

Here's The Thing!

Kid #1
Living or non-living?
Its teeth latch onto me.

Kid #2
Living or non-living?
Its legs hold it up.

Kid #3
Since it's a chair, it doesn't breathe
So it's a NON-LIVING thing.

Kid #2
Since it's a seed, it grows like a weed.
So it's a LIVING thing.

Kid #3
Living or non-living?
Its limbs are so strong.

Kid #4
Since it's a tree, it needs energy.
So it's a LIVING thing.

Kid #4
Living?
Non-living?

Does it exchange gases?
Make energy?
And grow?

Living or non-living?
Now you know!

More About Science

Chemical Reactions: A process where a set of substances undergo a chemical change to form a different substance, for example metal rusting or wood burning.

Erosion: Erosion occurs when the land is worn away over time by forces such as water, wind and ice.

Force and Motion: Force is the measurement of a push or pull on an object. Motion is the act or process of changing place.

Life Cycles: The developmental sequence an organism passes through over a life-time. Both plants and animals have life cycles.

Living/Non-living Things: Living things have basic needs to survive. They breathe, use energy, make waste, reproduce, and grow. Non-living things do not have any basic needs.

Magnetics/Magnets: Through an invisible, non-contact force field caused by their atomic properties, magnets either attract (pull together) or repel (push apart) other magnetic materials.

Seasons: The divisions of the year defined by changes in weather and the position of the earth in its orbit around the sun, typically winter, spring, summer and autumn (fall).

Sound: An energy that is caused by vibrations, heard by the ear, and interpreted by the mind to be noises, voices, or music.

Brain Waves: Electrical activity within the brain. These patterns of activity are then interpreted so that living beings can make sense of the world around them.

Structures: Something that is constructed in a particular way for a particular purpose. Each structure's constructive material has its own properties (i.e. how it looks, feels, and acts).

Sustainability: Living and making choices in such a way that the environment and future well-being of the planet and its creatures are not endangered.

Glossary

Botanic (buh-tan-ic): Made from a plant.

Carnivorous (kahr-niv-er-uhs): Able to trap and eat insects or small animals.

Germinate (jur-muh-neyt): When a seed begins to grow.

Gravity (grav-i-tee): A force that brings things together (e.g. a human is pulled to the earth).

Igneous Rock (ig-nee-uh-s): Rock formed from volcano lava or magma.

Larvae (lar-vee): Not-yet-grown insects or animals (e.g. grubs, caterpillars, or even tadpoles).

Pachyderm (pak-i-durm): A thick-skinned ungulate animal, such as an elephant or a rhinoceros.

Photosynthesize (foh-tuh-sin-thuh-sahyz): A process whereby, using the sun, plants create sugar and oxygen.

Pollination (pol-uh-ney-shuhn): The process whereby pollen is moved from one part of the plant (the anther) to another (the stigma), creating new seeds.

Pupae (pyoo-pee): Not-yet-grown, inactive insects or animals (e.g. chrysalises).

We would like to acknowledge the work of Drs. Xavier Fazio and Kamini Jai-pal-Jamani for their knowledge of science as they helped us vett this book.

Kari-Lynn Winters is a children's author, literacy researcher, and teacher. She has written/co-written several children's books, including *Hungry for Math*, *Gift Days*, and *Buzz About Bees*. She lives in St. Catharines, ON.

Lori Sherritt-Fleming, co-author of *Hungry for Math* and *aRHYTHMetic*, is an accomplished author, educator, and performer. She lives in Vancouver, BC.

Peggy Collins is an author, illustrator, and teacher. She's the illustrator of *Hungry for Math*, *In the Garden*, and *Tooter's Stinky Wish*. She lives near Kingston, ON.